FOR ELI

Published in the United States by Random House Children's Books,
a division of Random House, Inc., New York.
RANDOM HOUSE and colophon are registered trademarks of Random House, Inc.
www.randomhouse.com/kids
Educators and librarians, for a variety of teaching tools, visit us at
www.randomhouse.com/teachers
*Library of Congress Cataloging-in-Publication Data*
Kochalka, James.
Squirrelly Gray / James Kochalka. — 1st ed.
p. cm.
SUMMARY: When Squirrelly Gray loses his two front teeth, the Tooth Fairy's visit is just
the beginning of a night of surprises for the squirrel in his gray, colorless world.
ISBN 978-0-375-83975-7 (trade) — ISBN 978-0-375-93975-4 (lib. bdg.)
[1. Squirrels—Fiction. 2. Tooth fairy—Fiction. 3. Color—Fiction. 4. Stories in rhyme.] I. Title.
PZ8.3.K81513Squ 2007
[E]—dc22
2006031368

PRINTED IN CHINA   10 9 8 7 6 5 4 3 2 1   First Edition

# SQUIRRELLY GRAY

## James Kochalka

RANDOM HOUSE 🏠 NEW YORK

Jared
Laura Elizabeth

Once upon a boring time
When the world was gray,
A cold rain drizzled down upon
The forest every day.

The clouds were dark above the trees,
The ground was damp below.
There was no color anywhere,
And mud made walking slow.

Young Squirrelly Gray lived in a tree
And spent his time in bed,
Just watching static on TV,
Quite bored out of his head.

Squirrelly Gray, he wished to play,
So, like a silly goose,
He wiggled his front teeth for fun
Until they both were loose.

He wiggled them day after day,
And wiggled them some more.
He wiggled his front teeth until
They popped out on the floor!

He picked his teeth up carefully
And put them in his bed,
Underneath the pillow where
He laid his little head.

His eyelids, they grew heavier
As Squirrelly lay in wait.
He tried his best to stay awake,
But it got much too late.

Then in the middle of the night,
He woke up to a *yelp!*
He picked his little flashlight up
And ran outside to help.

Up in a sticky spider's web
The Tooth Fairy was stuck.
She hadn't seen it in the dark.
Of all the rotten luck!

Squirrelly Gray, he bravely tried
His very squirrelly best.
He freed the little fairy while
His heart thumped in his chest.

Before she flew away again
Collecting teeth that night,
She gave the squirrel a special gift
For helping set things right.

Squirrelly Gray could barely wait
To split the shell in two.
But with no teeth to crack the nut,
Just what could Squirrelly do?

Right then, at that very time,
And in that very place,
A fox strolled up to Squirrelly Gray,
A smirk upon his face.

The Hungry Fox, he flashed his teeth
On that most dismal night.
For it had been a good long while
Since Fox had eaten right.

Poor Squirrelly Gray, he trembled there,
Quite frozen stiff with fear,
While Hungry Fox just licked his lips,
And grinned from ear to ear.

The fox jumped up and swung his club
As quick as any knife.
But little Squirrelly Gray, he twitched.
That twitch, it saved his life!

And even though it wasn't what
The fox had meant to do,
His club came crashing down so hard
It split the nut in two!

Then magic colors tumbled out
From way down deep inside.
The clouds above, they all pulled back,
And up there in the sky . . .

A rainbow grew quite suddenly.
The first they'd ever seen!
It spread across the sky so blue,
Above the trees so green.

So what became of Hungry Fox
And of that club he had?
Did magic touch the fox's heart?
Was Hungry Fox less bad?

No, the Hungry Fox is just
As naughty as before.
But at least he cannot hurt
Young Squirrelly anymore.

For when he cracked the fairy's nut
And freed its magic power,
The Hungry Fox's great big club
Was turned into a flower.

Squirrelly laughed and kicked his heels
As he ran off to play,
While up above, the smiling sun
Shined brightly all the day.

And that is why the world we know
Is colorful and bright.
We all have one young squirrel to thank
For turning on the light!